Evil Portent

A science fiction novella, with a touch of humor

James Field

EVIL PORTENT

Bert turned the page of his alien invasion magazine and felt Olive's impatient eyes burn a hole into the back of his neck. Knowing his fiancé as he did, she had some gossip she wanted to pass on.

"Why do you read that rubbish?" she said.

Bert swung around, causing the chair to creak under his weight. Olive stood with her hands resting on her generous hips, her left foot tapping. "This here," said Bert, finger jabbing at his magazine, "is intellectual stuff, written by genuine professors about alien invasion and obstruction.

"Do you mean abduction, Bert?"

"Yeah, that's what I said, up-suction. I'm reading it because you don't like it when I read my Hulk comics or even Popeye. Popeye has a sweetheart called Olive, just like me and you, and when he eats spinach, his muscles grow so big that—"

"Stop it," screeched Olive.

Ah, what a divine sound, thought Bert. For one wild moment he considered giving her a mammoth cuddle, but he doubted she'd appreciate it under the circumstances. "Anyhow, these intellectual professors reckon aliens are roaming all over Earth."

"And you believe them?"

"Yeah, of course I do, otherwise I wouldn't be reading this rubbish, would I."

Olive's lavish make-up enhanced features broke into a smile. "Do I have your attention now?"

"Yeah," Bert closed his magazine and sighed. "Fire away."

"Have you seen the new neighbours at number three?"

Bert's house was number one in Flintstone Terrace. Olive's was the middle house at number two, which is where he now sat eating egg and bacon and studying the fantastic pictures in his magazine. Number three was at the terrace's other end. "No. What about them?"

"They're weird, spooky."

"Maybe they're aliens."

"Maybe I should clout you around the head. Anyway, Florence told me she—"

Bert shut his ears off and let his eyes drift back to his magazine. The pictures of wiry aliens with egg-shaped heads fascinated him. If he ever met one, he wondered what he'd say. Probably something like, "Welcome, mate. Please don't poop in the sink."

A knock at the front door made them both turn. "Come in," called Bert, even though it was Olive's house. "It ain't locked."

"Are your dogs safe?"

Bert recognised Chief Inspector Dobbs voice calling through the letterbox. Everyone was frightened of his two Alsatians, even though they'd never tear anybody's throat out unless he commanded them to. "No, me Chums are out back."

The door opened straight into the snug lounge. Three people stepped inside, each stopping to wipe their shoes on the Welcome mat: Vicar Bitter in his two-piece black suit and dog collar; Chief Inspector Dobbs in his yellow pullover and baggy trousers with turn-ups; and his wife, Florence, plump and younger-looking than her fifty-something years.

Their faces looked grave, and Bert wondered what he'd done wrong now. The last time they ganged up on him was to accuse him of being a pickpocket. He had been in his youth, good at it too, but not these days. These days he worked at the Cloud Estate as a security guard, and despite his brutal appearance, was mostly a model law-abiding citizen.

Olive lifted a pile of blankets and overstuffed cushions from the settee and dumped them on the floor. "Take a seat."

Florence nodded a greeting, bustled past her into the adjoining dining room, and sat at the table next to Bert. He shifted his bulk to give her room. The others followed and settled on the table's opposite side.

"I'll put the kettle on," said Olive, and headed for the kitchen. "I can't guess why you've come, but from the look of you, it must be some juicy gossip. Don't start until I get back."

With a pot of tea on the table and a plate piled with Bert's favourite cream eclairs in the table's centre, Olive dropped into the only remaining seat. "I'm ready. Bert, you can pour the tea."

The cups and saucers looked like doll's toys in his oversized mitts, but before he got as far as pouring the tea, Florence smacked the back of his hand and took over.

Chief Inspector Dobbs drummed his fingers and then spoke up. "Your new neighbours are causing concern in the local community. I believe they are criminals: dealers in drugs or child smuggling. Perhaps both."

"My concerns are far worse than yours," said Vicar Bitter, his layers of chins wobbling as he spoke. "They have horns, and I fear they worship Satan. Strange lights come from their windows all night long, and a teenager listened through their letterbox and claimed they were talking backwards."

Olive gasped and covered her mouth with her hands. Bert kept his eyes on the eclairs; he'd already selected the biggest.

"You're both being silly," said Florence. She lifted the teapot's lid and gave the brew a stir. "I'm the only one who's spoken to them and they're charming people. See here, the lady gave me a badge." She pointed to a disc on her hand-knitted cardigan, about the size of a coin. It glistened like a cat's eye, glittering with all the colours of the rainbow as she wiggled it. "I met them on the street late at night and the lady told me she was homeless. She had twelve children with her, none over four or five years old. I went straight to Mr Styles and got the keys for number three."

"Did you go in with her?" asked Olive.

"No, I didn't. But she was grateful."

"What did she look like?"

"It was dark. Difficult to see. She was small, a dwarf I would say."

Chief Inspector Dobbs coughed behind a clenched fist and plucked the eclair Bert had his eye on. "You and Olive," he said to Bert, "are their closest neighbour. You can do us all a favour, Bert, by keeping a watch on them. Go and visit, check them out, and report to me."

"You want me to spy on her?" said Bert. He didn't like the sound of that. People were entitled to their privacy, that's how it should be. What business was it of any other?

"Yes, as much for her own safety as anything else. Everybody in the hamlet has taken a disliking to her and her kids. Some of the older youths have thrown stones at her house, and adults are talking about setting fire to it."

That changed matters for Bert. One goings-on he couldn't stand was mobbing and bullying. If he caught anyone throwing stones at her house, he'd break their wrist. If anyone so much as lit a cigarette in front of her house, he'd ram the whole packet down their throat. All the same, the idea of visiting her didn't appeal to him. "Why can't you go?"

"The vicar and I went to her house before coming here, but she didn't answer the door. I know she's in there because she peeked at us from behind the curtain."

"What about Florence? Seeing as she's already spoken to them, why can't she go?"

"Because," said Florence, passing the cups of tea around and helping herself to the next biggest eclair, "my silly husband thinks it's too dangerous." She blew Chief Inspector Dobbs a kiss.

A flush crept across Dobbs cheeks, and he made a rush job of blowing the kiss back. "I'll not have her exposed to unnecessary risks."

"Okay," said Bert. He couldn't understand what all the fuss was about. How could a midget woman and a bunch of kids put such a fright into people? "I'll go first thing in the morning. You lot must have scared the poor woman half to death. But what makes you think she'll open her door to me? My ugly mug scares the crap out of people."

"I know," said Florence. She tore the glittering badge from her cardigan and passed it to Bert. "Take this and say I vouch for you. Once people get to know you, they soon find you're the sweetest creature on Earth."

***

Next morning, on a grey and drizzly day that kept most people snuggled between their sheets, Bert trundled to the stable with his two Alsatians, his Chums as he liked to call them, to tend his horse, Bigfoot. The stable owner had sold the horse to Bert at a favourable price because it was so cantankerous it wouldn't let anybody near it, let alone ride it.

Bigfoot was one of the stable owner's experiments. He'd crossed a cold-blooded carthorse with a hot-blooded Arabian. He hoped the result would be a warm-blooded workhorse, but ended with a hot-blooded stallion that weighed just over a ton and towered two metres tall.

Despite Bert's fierce appearance, children and animals adored him, and Bert was so big and heavy that Bigfoot was the only horse strong enough to carry him. To everyone's astonishment, the two unredeemable souls had bonded at first meeting.

After tethering Bigfoot outside number three Flintstone Terrace, and commanding his Chums to stay put and wait for him, Bert tapped on his new neighbour's front door. He reckoned they must be in, because he could see the curious light everyone talked about, throbbing behind the curtains. The stark light, like the full moon on a frosty night, faded and grew in the same rhythm as a person in deep sleep.

A thought crossed Bert's sluggish mind. Florence hadn't mentioned anything about the new neighbours having luggage or bags with them. Did they have food? If not, Bert had plenty he could share. After one more unresponsive knock, he trundled around to the rear of Flintstone Terrace and entered the back lane. The lane ran parallel to the houses, their gardens on the lane's other side. Lawn covered all of number three's garden, making it easy for the tenant to keep tidy. Ankle deep weeds covered most of it.

The three houses' backyards were also similar: a row of bunkers for coal and coke along one side, an outside toilet and an entrance to the kitchen on the other. Like his own house at number one, this kitchen door only had a latch and a bolt on the inside to hold it locked. Tentatively, Bert tried the latch. It lifted, and the bolt was clear, so he pushed the door open and called. "Cooey, it's only me, Bert, your friendly neighbour. Can I come in?"

The sound of whimpering greeted Bert, and when they still didn't answer, he stepped inside. From the kitchen, he crept across the living room and into the front room. In a corner, huddled beneath the window, he found the group.

The minuscule woman stared at him as if the devil confronted her. Her eyes were placed far apart on each side of her head with a broad nose-bridge between them. The eyes moved in different directions, and the pupils weren't round, but oval, like a goat's. A curly mop of grey hair partially covered two bony nubs on her prominent forehead. Her mouth and jaws were more or less normal.

Bert counted twelve children. The woman clutched her arms around two of them, their faces buried in her chest. The others hid behind her back, crying, not daring to look at him.

The only furniture in the room was a tatty three-piece suite and a shoddy sideboard. In the middle of the timeworn-carpeted floor, lay the object that emitted the curious light. About the size of a shoebox, it reminded Bert of the inside workings of an old-fashioned wind-up clock. Instead of springs, cogs and spindles trapped between two metal plates, microchips floated, as if suspended in a purple gooey liquid that throbbed with a million points of light.

Bert raised his palms to show he meant no harm, but the woman screeched at him in a language he'd never heard before, Arabic maybe, spoken backwards.

Worried the poor woman might blow a fuse, Bert found the badge Florence had given him and slapped it on his breast. The badge had no pin, but its backside was rough like Velcro, and it stuck tight to his T-shirt.

A jumble of noises rattled through his brain, like listening to a party political debate played too fast and cymbals crashing every so often. Then, behind the noise, he realised the woman spoke English to him. He shook his head to clear it and listened.

"Don't kill us. We mean no harm. I broke my Doodad, or we'd leave."

"I'm here to help," said Bert. "I ain't going to hurt you." He pointed to the flashing contraption on the carpet. "Is that the Doodad you mean?"

"Yes. We're marooned in this hellhole world forever."

Bert stopped breathing. "This world?"

"Haven't you savages heard of other worlds?"

"You mean like a home for dwarfs with Down's syndrome?"

"No, I mean like other inhabited planets out in the universe."

A penny dropped within Bert and he realized these people had escaped from a loony bin. He thought it best to humour her. "Some people believe, but most don't." He shuffled his feet and scratched his backside. "I'm one of those who believe."

The woman sobbed. "Worse and worse. Oh, if only we hadn't come."

"Well, why did you?"

"To escape the Guardians. But this world is no safer. You creatures are a race of fierce, egoistic beasts who kill animals for their meat."

Definitely a loony, thought Bert, escaped from an asylum somewhere. Time to phone Florence for help; she possessed almost as much gumption as his best friend, Alf. "When did you last eat?" he asked as he plucked his smartphone from his back pocket.

The woman flinched and drew her children to her breast. "Don't shoot," she whimpered. "We're so small, there's hardly any meat on us."

Bert scratched his head. No doubt. Just plain nuts. "This is a phone," he explained, drawing the words out and holding it to his ear to demonstrate. "I'm going to call for help."

A wave of relief washed over the woman's face, but only enough to give her the courage to speak calmer. "A phone. Can I see it?"

"Yeah. Take a look. It's harmless." He held it at arm's length and the woman snatched it from his hand. "Hey," he said, "Don't do that." But it was too late. She tore the back cover from the phone, ripped out the battery, prodded at its workings with what resembled a crochet hook until her palm contained a jumble of fragments.

"It weren't a gun," said Bert, dejectedly. "You didn't have to ruin it, and if you didn't want me to call for help, all you had to do was to say."

The woman didn't answer. Instead, she sifted through the bits as if hunting for lice. Then she pinched up one black piece, dumped the rest of his ruined phone on the carpet, and picked up the Doodad. With the Doodad in one hand and the part from his phone in the other, she slipped the part into the Doodad. Immediately, the gadget's harsh light stopped throbbing.

All held their breath and stared at the Doodad. Pricks of various coloured pinpoint lights danced and ticked. Then it peeped and the purple goo settled into a soft, faint, glow.

With a jubilant cheer, the woman bounced to her feet and clapped her hands. "It works," she said.

"What works?"

"Can't you see? The Doodad. We can return to our own world."

The children danced and pranced with as much boisterousness as a pack of excited Billy Goats.

"Wait and watch," said the woman. Bouncing from foot to foot, eyes gleaming, she placed the gadget back on the floor.

Without warning, the air above it warped, like a heat haze, even though the room was freezing. Looking into the haze was like peering into a fire while daydreaming. Only there were no flames, just the vague impression of a black hole.

Bert stared at the patch of distorted air. It grew larger and more distinct, and he spotted odd translucent shapes eddying within it. A dull pressure made his ears ache, and a drop of sweat slid down the hollow of his throat, leaving a cold track.

The hazy hole had no outer boundary; it simply hung in midair, the entrance to a tunnel leading to an unearthly distance. Every muscle in Bert's body seized, pressure built in his ears, and the hiss of piercing static made his teeth cringe. The tunnel's depth pulsed like a black gulping throat, and the static hiss grew louder, wavering in pitch.

"Come," said the woman, suddenly by his side and tugging on his hand. "Come with us."

"Where?"

"To our world."

Bert, still hypnotised by the tunnel and fascinated by the notion of other worlds, staggered along beside her. They stepped inside, its depths shrinking and widening like the gullet of a black snake.

Ahead of him, he saw the woman and her twelve children melt into clouds of powder and the tunnel inhale them. It was the weirdest sensation Bert had ever experienced. The front edge of his bulk crumbled into dust and vanished into the tunnel as if dragged along by a tornado. Instinctively, he held his head back, watching, but in the same instant his vision blurred and a wall of soft foam in his back drove him forward. There was a sharp sting of pain as if blunt needles stabbed every nerve in his body. Before he had time to cry out, his flesh and bones gained substance again, as if he'd just woken from a nightmare and realised all was right with the world.

Except he wasn't lying in bed; he wobbled on his feet on the top of a green hill.

Below the hilltop, a village of flimsy huts and cabins nestled beside a rushing river. In every direction, Bert noted forests and fields of bamboo. A warm breeze, laden with the scent of tobacco, chafed the bamboo's feathery leaves, wavering between rest and motion.

"What's that?" asked Bert, pointing to a distant hill higher than the others. A black tower dominated its summit. It looked alien and out of place.

"Can you see the Citadel from here?"

"Can't you?"

Both the woman's eyes focused in that direction. "No, it is too far away."

"And what's that?" Bert pointed to another construction of grey stone on a ridge on the village's other side."

"That is the abbey where the terror-stricken monks live."

Bert noticed his palms sweated and wiped them on his T-shirt. "Where the heck are we?"

The woman's two eyes swivelled in all directions, as if uneasy. "I think we're safe for the moment."

"Yeah, that's good, but where are we?"

"I must take you to the Elder's house. He'll explain everything." Without further word, the woman bent to pick up a Doodad similar to the one they'd left behind and set off down the hill, heading for the village on her dumpy little legs.

Bert tagged along beside her, taking advantage of the sluggish pace to absorb his new surroundings. Temple bells chimed through the mystic, potent sunlight; frogs croaked in muddy ditches; dwarf-sized women came from the fields, with a song on their thin red lips and wicker baskets laden with bamboo tips on their heads.

They glared at Bert as if he were a monster, taking a wide berth or darting into their hovels.

The villagers had constructed most of their huts from thick bamboo canes. There were no vehicles and only hard-packed dirt paths. It reminded him of pictures he'd seen of undiscovered tribes in South America's rain forests, except here it looked as though they'd cleared most of the forest to cultivate fields of bamboo.

A handful of stone-built constructions, twice as large as the huts, were sprinkled haphazardly throughout the village. They headed for one of these.

Bert ducked inside and wiped his feet on a mat made of fibres. Doors and windows were simple open gaps with cloth hanging across the doors. Bamboo shutters in the windows did little to keep the sun out. After the sweltering heat outdoors, the cool cave-like room made Bert shiver and he shoved his hands into his pockets.

A little prune of a man sat cross-legged on the dirt floor. When he caught sight of Bert, squeezing through the door and standing with his head and shoulders bent beneath the low ceiling, he leapt effortlessly to his feet and backed into a corner.

Apart from his widespread eyes, the Elder had squished his facial features into a tight knot, making him look like an amazed chipmunk. "What are you?" he asked.

"Me name's Bert. Pleased to meet you." He held his hand out and the little man cringed even further into the corner. "I ain't going to hurt you." Tired of bending his head, Bert flopped to the floor and leant back on his arms.

The alien woman stepped from behind Bert's back. When the Elder saw her, his expression flitted between relief, joy, confusion, and anger. "Troublemaker. What have you done?"

"I bring you a Bert. He witnessed the tunnel, so I kidnapped him."

"Is a Bert safe?"

"The Berts are violent meat-eaters, but I believe this one is peaceful."

"Why do you keep saying we're meat eaters," said Bert. "Some of us are vegans. They only eat leaves and seeds and stuff."

"I say you are meat eaters," said the woman, "because your eyes are close together and focused to judge distance. All hunters of meat share that trait. Our eyes move independently of each other. A common trait of all hunted animals, forever on the watch for the hunters."

"Vegans must be the superior species on your planet," said the Elder. "Do Vegans have the wide-spread eyes of the hunted?"

Bert shook his head. "No, but they fart a lot."

"Go then!" said the Elder, his finger jabbing at the woman. "Leave the Doodad here. I will talk with this Bert and reprimand you later."

The woman bowed and hurried away.

"Sit!" said the Elder.

"I am sitting," said Bert.

The Elder's eyes swivelled this way and that as if wondering how he could squeeze around Bert if he needed to escape. Bert felt sorry for the timid little wise man and offered his friendliest smile.

"You are confused?"

Bert wasn't sure if it was a statement or a question. "I don't know where I am if that's what you mean."

"You are on a planet called Ewepiter, in a village called Lambdon."

Careful to keep the smirk on his face, Bert shook his head. "Never heard of them."

A slow grin softened the Elder's panic, and his posture slumped. "Are you hungry, Bertling, thirsty?"

"I'm starving and me throat's parched. A pint or two of beer would work wonders."

The Elder lifted the lid of a large saucepan that balanced on a flat metal box. "I'll make some porridge for you." He scooped a handful of dry bamboo tips from a sack and tossed them into the pan. Then he added another handful, turned to glance at Bert, and added two more. After filling water and a handful of white powder Bert assumed was salt, he put the lid back on and tapped the side of the metal box with a finger. "Two minutes," he said.

All the while, the Elder kept one eye on Bert, the other on the pan. "There's water in the barrel by your right elbow," he said.

A ladle hung on the barrel with cups of various sizes stacked neatly on a low table by its side. Bert chose the largest and gulped four cupfuls before his tongue came unstuck from the roof of his mouth. The metal box peeped, and when the Elder lifted the saucepan lid, steam belched out.

"Blimey, mate, how did you cook that?" Bert scratched his bald head. He didn't see any flames beneath the pan or electric wires anywhere.

"It is part of the remnants of our technology, like the translator you wear on your T-shirt, and this cooker, and those Doodads. Only a few of us retain the wisdom of how these contrivances work. I am not one of those, so I cannot explain."

"Got any cream and sugar?" asked Bert as the Elder nudged a bowl of porridge in his direction and edged away again.

"No."

Bert blew on his spoon and, careful not to burn his tongue, took a nibble. He shuddered and gagged. The porridge was the most disgusting he'd tasted in his life: earthy, woody, like mild water chestnuts but with a bitter tang. "Blimey, mate, you've got to be joking. Ain't you got nothing else?"

"No."

"What do you mean, no? Is this all you eat?"

"Yes."

"No wonder you're all so small. Sorry, but I can't eat this."

Terror filled the Elder's face. "You're just like the Guardians. You crave meat. You prefer to eat us."

"No," said Bert, and hurriedly spooned porridge into his gob, his cheeks blowing out like balloons. "Look, I'm eating this yummy stuff." He found it almost impossible to swallow and spat globs of the creamy sludge as he spoke, but he kept spooning it in. "Mmm! lovely."

Bert stopped eating, set the bowl by his side, pinched his nose, and swallowed. He grimaced and coughed, then smiled and smacked his lips. The Elder watched him closely. It pained Bert to see the little man so frightened. "Look, I ain't going to eat you. Not any of you. It's true

I eat meat where I come from, but they're only farm animals."

"To the Guardians, we are only farm animals."

There it was again, a reference to the Guardians. "What do you mean? Who are these Guardians?"

A new wave of terror made the Elder shake. "The evilest monsters in the universe. They are from a different planet, and they have an open tunnel like the one you came through. They farm us and eat us."

"Can't you close the tunnel?"

"We could, easily, but they guard the Doodad."

"Where?"

"In a tower they erected on a hill near to here."

Bert nodded. "The Citadel I could see when I got here?"

"Yes."

Bert held a palm up to stop the Elder from piling on more misery. "Look, as soon as I've finished this delicious porridge I'll pop back to me own planet and leave you in peace."

"You can never leave."

It took a moment for Bert's brain to register what the Elder had said. Even then, he thought he must have heard wrong. "Did you say 'never leave'?"

"Yes."

"Why?"

"Because the Guardians know we have opened a tunnel to another planet: your planet. If they find the Doodad, they will open the tunnel and invade your world."

A sharp, disgusted snort broke from Bert. "Our people aren't passive like you lot. If those Guardians come to our world, we'd clobber them good and proper."

"Perhaps, but their weapon technology is awesome." He made a snide gesture to the knife hanging in Bert's belt. "They have a hand-held ray gun whose beam destroys anything it touches. One sweep would wipe out this entire village."

Bert raised his eyebrows and gave a glassy stare. "Listen, mate, I can't live here. I'll starve to death."

"My friend," said the Elder, "I am sorry and will punish the woman who kidnapped you." He offered a deep sigh. "The day the Guardians discover you they will kill you. But isn't that better than they follow you back to your planet and kill or enslave your entire population of Berts and Vegans?"

Irritation flared in Bert. Rather than do or say something he might regret, he crawled out of the Elder's hut on hands and knees. He wanted to go home to Olive, to his Chums the Alsatians, and his horse, Bigfoot.

In his younger days, Bert had been thief, good at it too. Someway or another, as sure as his name was Bert, he'd snitch the Doodad from the Elder's hut and transport himself back to Earth. As soon as he re-entered number three Flintstone Terrace, all he needed to do was turn the Doodad off. End of problem.

The alien woman who'd kidnapped him waited outside. "Don't be angry," she said. "Wait for me while the Elder dishes out my punishment. Then I'll take you to my cottage."

Two minutes later, she was out again, her face ashen. "Come."

"What's the punishment?"

"Food rationing for three days. Half measure."

"That ain't so bad. You can have my share."

They trekked through the village of well-spaced bamboo huts and arrived at another stone-built house, not as large or austere as the Elder's, but inviting and cosy. This one had a proper, solid door. Bert crouched, but could still feel the ceiling scrub his bald head. A small man greeted the woman with a big hug, and tears flowed easily from both.

"This is the father of my children," said the alien woman.

"Welcome," said the Alien Father. "Are you hungry?"

Unlike the Elder, he appeared unafraid of Bert. For an Ewepitarian he was tall, almost reaching Bert's belly button. The horny nodes on his forehead were more prominent than the woman's, and his features hinted at a strong character. There were no chairs big enough for Bert, so he sat cross-legged on the floor, his head on a level with the Alien Father's head. "Depends what you're offering."

"Bamboo porridge. There is nothing else."

"Then I ain't hungry."

"Sit!" said the Alien Father.

"I am sitting."

The Alien Father stared at the floor, hands clasped. "You are here through no fault of your own." He reached out to touch Bert, then pulled back as if not worthy, or perhaps nervous. "I owe you an explanation."

"Too blinking right you do."

"Many hundreds of years ago, our people dominated Ewepiter in their billions. They drove almost all other species to extinction. Food was short, pollution was high, and our world was dying. We needed to find a new planet to live on, so we built the..." he scratched his head, concentrating, then shrugged, "the Doodads."

"The gadget that makes the tunnel between planets?"

"Yes. When we activate a tunnel, we only have limited control over where it opens. The planet must be hospitable: breathable atmosphere, comfortable temperature, compatible gravity, and so on; but we cannot tell what life forms live there. When we pass through the tunnel, we anchor the other end by placing a Doodad there too. Unfortunately, our first and only attempt opened on the Guardian's planet. They invaded us, confiscated our technology, and farmed us for the meat of our bodies."

"Why did you come to my planet then?"

"On all Ewepiter, we have just two Doodads left. We've kept them hidden all these years and never used them.

When the Guardians came to our village a few days ago to round up the young, I ordered the mother of my children to gather all the infants in our village and take them through the tunnel to safety. If lucky, she might have found a planet where we could all escape. Alas, this time also, it opened on a useless, hazardous world, and now you are here and can never return."

Bert noticed his hands clench. "Why not?"

"Because we closed the tunnel and hid the Doodad."

"So, I'm a prisoner, is that it?"

The Alien Father cringed, and his voice turned husky. "You're a guest,"

"Anyway, what about the Doodad that's left behind on my world, in number-three Flintstones Terrace?"

"Lost forever."

Bert shook his head slightly. "We know where it is, so it ain't lost." He scrunched his eyebrows together. "What about if you turned the Doodad on again at this end?"

"The tunnel would open, but you will never find it and use it, and neither must the Guardians. The next time it opens, the Guardians will find it easily and invade your world, and the fate of the Berts and the Vegans will be the same as Ewepitarians." He spread his dinky legs, rested his hands on his hips, and gave Bert a harsh squint. "The destiny of your planet is in your hands."

Cogs swirled in Bert's brain. "What about if you smash the Guardian's Doodad? The one that opens to their world?"

"That is why we call them Guardians. They guard the Doodad in their citadel on the hill. Nobody dares go there."

"What? Nobody?"

"I tried to organise a surveillance group once, but everyone said I was mad."

"So you just let the Guardians piss all over you?"

"What else can we do?"

"Fight back."

The Alien Father visibly shook in his boots. "I'd give anything to be as big and strong as you, Bert. Then I wouldn't be so frightened of them."

"Why not let me go home and come back with a pile of weapons?" Bert drew his knife, the eight-inch blade flashing in the light. "I only use this as a toothpick. With a few bazookas we'll soon stop those pesky Guardians. Then we can all live happily ever after."

"How can I trust you'll return?"

That was a good question. The answer was simple. He'd return because it was the right thing to do. If it came to a fight, he'd die for his buddies, even new buddies like these kindly little people who ate nothing but repulsive grunge. He had his moral values, too. He'd never allow bullies to lay a finger on children or animals, and he wouldn't let space invaders continue to ravish this fine world for all the money in China. "If I didn't come back to help you, I'd never forgive myself."

"No, forget it. It can never be. Our people are not warriors. In our millions of years of evolution, there has never been a war. Besides, the Guardians would follow you and ravish your planet."

That was a problem Bert would sort out if and when it should happen. Right now, he needed the little man on his side. "You were brave enough to go against the Elder's rules and open a new tunnel to my planet."

"Yes, and look what trouble I've caused. The Guardians are keeping an extra eye on us when all we want is inconspicuous peace."

"Don't look so glum, you saved the lives of all your children."

"No, I didn't. The guardians will come again, and when they see you, they'll punish us. Oh, woe is me."

Just then, a hammering of fists erupted on his door, and the poor man almost fainted.

"Open up," they heard voices cry.

The Alien Father closed his eyes and summoned a deep breath, holding it in. Turning his head a fraction, as though straining to understand the voices, he uttered a soft curse and tutted. "I feared the Guardians were here, but it's simply the villagers."

Bert's stomach growled, he noticed a headache coming on, and if he didn't eat something soon he worried he'd lose his powers of reasoning. The crowd's urgent mumbling outside and the loud thudding on the door drove him crazy. "Can't you see what they want?"

"They sound panicky," said the Alien Father.

"Well, at least they ain't hungry. Are you going to tell them to go away, or shall I?"

The Alien Father squeezed past Bert, rushed to the door, and tore it open. "What is it?" he asked, a quiver in his voice.

Bert peered over his head and narrow shoulders and saw the whole yard swarmed with little people. As far as he could see, the entire village had gathered. The Elder headed the group, his fist still raised and ready to bash against the door. "The Guardians are coming in their hundreds," he said, and his knees rattled in his baggy shorts. He pointed to the citadel on the mountain. "They're firing cannons and hurling death rays in every direction."

The Alien Father stopped to listen, then darted out to see for himself. Bert pressed his shoulders through the opening; rose to his full six-foot and five-inches, stretched his back, and let out a groan of relief. The villagers must have seen him as an overgrown gorilla because they yelped and scuttled to a prudent distance.

Even on Earth, Bert's fierce appearance had the same effect on people, so he ignored their reaction and peered across to the distant hill with its citadel. In that direction, the heavens had turned black with the bruise of thick angry clouds. The darkening sky rumbled worse than Bert's empty stomach and jagged silver flashes jabbed at the coming night. A cool breeze caressed his bare arms and a lone drop of rain kissed his bald head. "It's only a storm." Bert could see his new friend was uncertain.

The Alien Father tilted his head from side to side, weighing the possibilities. "It could be thunder and lightning, but it could also be a new offensive by the Guardians. In times like this, when we've opened a port to a new world, who can tell?"

"We take no chances," said the Elder. "This house has an underground shelter," he called to the crowd. "We take refuge here."

Like a bunch of frightened mice, the villagers surged to the Alien Father's house. The Alien Father stood in the entrance, arms stretched, blocking them out. "Not so fast," he said.

The crowd bowled the Alien Father aside and stormed in. He tried to protest, but nobody took any notice. Outside, the distant rumbling grew louder. "It's only a storm," said the Alien Father. "More violent than normal, but that's all it is."

"No," insisted the Elder. "You have angered the Guardians by hiding the children and opening a tunnel to another planet. They're amassing in large numbers, and soon they'll be here to kill us all." He jabbed a finger in the Alien Father's chest. "You brought them, you shelter us. Isn't that fair?"

It would have been easy for Bert to stop them from occupying the Alien Father's house. He only needed to plonk his bulk in the doorway, and if the Elder dared to poke him in the chest, he'd snap his finger off. It wasn't exactly his intuition that told him not to interfere, more his hunger that had made his brain too sluggish to react.

Bert peered in at them through the open door. The house was so crowded that everyone sat side by side on the floor, men, women, and children, leaving no room for him. They'd even occupied the bedrooms. The underground shelter was nothing more than a cool pantry, filled with sacks of bamboo shoots.

"Anybody got anything decent to eat?" called Bert. It was soon clear nobody had food with them. In their hurried fright, they'd forgotten to bring any.

The villagers hadn't been sitting long in the Alien Father's house before a cry went out for drink, and another for food. "We eat what we find," called the Elder, and all cheered in agreement. "We can't starve to death in this hour of refuge."

They opened cupboards, placed a huge pan on the heater box, and prepared bamboo-tip porridge in vast quantities. Bert would have settled for a bucket of popcorn, or a raw carrot, or even boiled spinach to make his muscles grow like Popeye; anything but that disgusting porridge.

The Alien Father tottered out of his house and sat next to Bert in the humid warmth. He spoke through his teeth with forced restraint. "Am I not master in my own home?" he said. "This is how we are. We flock together when frightened, and with the enemy out of sight and hearing, all we think about is food. My food."

Bert patted him on the arm. "It'll be okay, you'll see." It occurred to him this was the first physical contact he'd made with any of them, and the tough little guy didn't react worse than stiffening and going still. "If you let me go home, I'll bring some seeds with me too. You could grow corn and oranges and potatoes and all sorts of stuff that tastes delicious."

With a probing gaze, the Alien Father cast a glance into Bert's face. He wet his lips and swallowed hard. "I'll think about it." Then, with hesitant steps, he went back into his house.

With everybody slurping their porridge, conversation settled to a mumble. Bert sat outside, and many thoughts came and went in his sluggish brain. Thunder still rumbled up on the mountain, and he didn't understand how the little people mistook the storm for an invasion. Hadn't they felt the few drops of rain? The idiots were so hysterical that he couldn't imagine how to convince them otherwise.

Such behaviour irritated Bert. Wasn't there ever a time in their past when they had more guts? The only one who showed signs of bravery was the Alien Father, and even that didn't amount to much.

A hard smile came to his lips. He needed release for his frustration, and the little people needed shaking up. Glancing about, he singled out a boulder about the size of a briefcase and tested its weight. He guessed eighty kilos. With his teeth gritted, and muscles cramping under the strain of holding it above his head, he stumbled the few steps back to the house. There, grunting in a last supreme effort, he tossed the boulder against the side of the house with all his might.

It pummelled the building like a cannonball, and inside he heard plaster and cement fall from the wall and ceiling. "Yeah, now the weedy little runts have something to think about other than porridge and water."

The door burst open and the Elder dashed through like the wind. "Save yourself those that can," he screeched. "The Guardians are attacking."

Wild terror had broken out in the house. All wanted to escape at once, but in their panic, they stuck in the door frame and couldn't get out or back in. Bert gave a nudge here and a tug there sufficient to untangle the jam and clear the way.

"One at a time," said Bert, acting as a doorman. "And watch out for the children."

Like a flock of frightened rabbits, they scattered from the house and fled up through the woods towards the hills. Panic gripped the Alien Father too, and with a child under each arm, he raced up the path to join the others. "To the hills, to the hills," he shouted. "This is the end of Lambdon."

Bert trotted by his side, the path rising so steeply he soon gasped for breath. "Where are you off to?"

"To the temple in the hills."

Bert recalled seeing it in the opposite direction of the Guardian's citadel. "Are you going to be any safer there?"

"The guardians are hurling grenades at us." He glared at Bert, his face one big question mark. "You were outside, didn't you see it?"

"I ain't built for running," said Bert, ignoring the awkward question. He stopped, leant forward with hands on his knees, and spat.

"Every one of us must reach the monastery. You too, Bert. The Guardians will raise the village to the ground."

Bert scratched behind his ear and then tapped at the translator-badge fastened to his T-shirt. He didn't understand how something could be raised to the ground. Surely the Alien Father meant flattened to the ground?

"I'll stay," he called as the Alien Father mingled with the last of the villagers and disappeared from view among the trees. "If the Guardians come, which I doubt, they'll have me to deal with." He spat again. He didn't suppose anyone heard his final words.

With shoulders slumped, Bert traipsed back to Lambdon. He missed his two Alsatians and his horse, Bigfoot. They must miss him too, he thought, and while he was trapped on this strange alien planet, who would see to them? Nobody, apart from his buddy, Alf, dared to go near them. But Alf wasn't fond of animals and probably wouldn't think to feed them or bother to groom Bigfoot properly.

Bert gave a little whimper of mirth. The first time Bigfoot allowed him to climb onto its back, Bert faced the wrong way. It happened next time, too. He'd never ridden a horse, but when The Stable's owner, Mr Styles, finished laughing, he taught Bert all about it. And Bert learnt fast. Despite his bulk, and after years of sparing with Alf, his coordination, balance, and agility were exceptional.

Bigfoot was the most majestic and proud creature Bert had ever known, and they soon trusted and loved each other. To ride Bigfoot was thrilling and nerve-racking at the same time. It made Bert feel as though he had superpowers, and it wasn't long before they played and pranced and performed tricks like a circus act.

He stumbled now into the alien's deserted village and wondered if he'd ever see his friends again. When he reached the Alien Father's yard, he stuck his hands in his pockets, and gazed about. A light bulb suddenly glowed dimly in his head. The villagers had all fled. Little did he think he'd be walking here as the only living person in the settlement.

His chest felt lighter and a slow smile crossed his lips. With the little people gone, he could find the Doodad and tunnel off back to Earth.

The last place he'd seen the Doodad was in the Elder's house, so that's where he started his search. He found it where the Elder had discarded it, on the floor next to his chair. With his mouth gaping wide, he stared at it, dumbfounded by the Elder's carelessness and his own great fortune.

He carried the gadget back to the Alien Father's house and rotated it this way and that, hunting for a start button. There were no buttons, but determined to make it work, he studied the contraption more closely. It was a square-shaped object about the size of a chunky hardback book with firm green jelly sandwiched between two thin metal plates.

A jelly sandwich, the thought made his mouth water.

Jelly and metal? Not really. The materials embodied a strange, snakeskin texture he didn't recognise. There were no markings on the metal surfaces; both were a dull grey, but one side felt warmer than the other. And the jelly can't have been jelly all the way through because miniature stars and constellations hurried about within, blinking and flashing like a miniature galaxy.

Bert prodded the jelly, stroked it, tapped it first with one finger and then with two, and then repeated the process on both metal plates. Nothing happened. No tunnel opened.

He shook it, twirled it, flipped it like a coin, balanced it on his head, and then stopped to think. What had the Alien Mother done to make it work? She'd dropped a piece from his ruined mobile phone into the Doodad, said it was working, and placed it on the floor.

For starters, how did she drop the piece into the workings? Bert found no opening so he ignored that part and carried on to the next. He held it in both hands, lifted it to his face and said firmly, "It's working." Then he set it on the floor. Still nothing.

He lifted his hands in an "I give up" gesture, stuffed the Doodad in a hole in the stone wall, and jammed a dislodged stone on top. With the Doodad hidden, Bert stalked away from the village and headed for the hill temple.

When at last he reached the temple, he was so exhausted he could hardly stand. The villagers were in no better shape; some had lost hats, some had lost shoes. One man's braces had snapped and his trousers hung around his knees.

It was midafternoon, and all were so weary that they huddled on the temple's stone-cold floor and dozed. Couples and children clung to one another for warmth. The others clutched themselves and shivered.

The temple was dome-shaped, built from chalky white stone. Large by comparison to the villager's homes, Bert could stand erect under its roof and didn't need to duck while passing through the arched doorways. Doors and windows were mere holes in the stonework, offering no protection from the chilly breeze.

Bert strutted in, and the Alien Father rushed to greet him, a smile beaming on his face.

"You're still alive," said the Alien Father, rubbing sleep from his eyes.

"Yeah," said Bert. "What did you expect? You left the village deserted and there ain't no sign of the Guardians."

"But we witnessed them in the hills," said the Alien Father in self-defence. "They threw a grenade at us. The whole building shook."

"Mini earthquake, and the ruckus on the hill was a local thunderstorm. That's what you so-called men scampered from. I'm disappointed in you."

The Alien Father sunk his head. "You are right. We have behaved like scared children." But he pulled himself together and demanded attention from his kinfolk. "Everyone back to your daily lives. It was merely a thunderstorm we ran from, not a raid of Guardians."

The Elder squeezed to the front of the crowd and faced the Alien Father. There was no sign of aggression in his posture, but his tone rippled with authority. "How do you know?"

"Because I said so." Bert towered above the Elder and he jabbed a podgy finger at his face. "Wanna make something of it?"

The Elder backed off two paces. The villagers stirred anxiously.

"I waited until the storm blew away," said Bert. "Nobody or nothing came to your village. Go to your homes and stop acting like a load of stupid sheep."

Some villagers groaned, others laughed, but when they heard what Bert had to say they understood they'd acted rashly. With jokes and commotion, the crowd strolled back to their valley.

"Don't judge us harshly," said the Alien Mother as she passed Bert. Children clutched at her skirt and her gaze darted anxiously between them. "The Guardian's threat is real. They snatch children from the entire planet and we have many in our village of a ripe age. One day soon they will come, and we can't stop them." Tears welled in her eyes.

"I'm sorry." Bert stared at the floor, hands hanging by his side. Women's tears always brought him to his knees. "It's just that I'm hungry and I want to go home." He sniffed. "I'm ashamed of meself for going on at you poor people. Of course those Guardians terrify you." His muscles tightened and he spread his stance. "Don't you fear none. You aren't alone. As long as I'm here, ain't nobody going to harm the kids."

"At least," said the Elder, shooing his people along, "we have tested our evacuation strategy."

***

A short while after Bert and the Alien Father had returned home and made themselves comfortable, a frantic banging pounded at their door. The Elder burst in, gasping for breath. "The Doodad is missing. Somebody stole it."

Bert whistled and gazed into the ceiling.

The Alien Father blinked at him. "Bert?"

"How should I know?" Bert shrugged.

"Because you were here, alone."

"Not all the time I wasn't. I came up to the temple with you lot."

A look of understanding crossed the Elder's face. "The Guardians have been here." His face grew grim. "They've found the Doodad." He nodded, sighed, and an air of sorrow replaced his other expressions. He almost patted Bert's arm. "I'm sorry, but it means they will invade your world of Bertlings and Vegans. I should've hidden the it better."

"Yeah," said Bert, "leaving it next to your chair like that was—." He clamped his mouth shut and cussed, but the Elder didn't react. Rather, he finally combated his terror of

Bert, reached up, slapped his arm in commiseration, and went away.

The Alien Father wasn't so easily fooled and he challenged Bert. "If you damaged it, you've taken all hope of escape from us."

"Weren't me what took it." There was no conviction in Bert's meek voice, and he hung his head. "I want to go home. Why should I break it?"

"I'm not saying you ruined it on purpose, but it's fragile."

"Oh!" said Bert, recalling how clumsily he'd handled it. But he was an optimistic sort of bloke and was confident it wasn't broken. The reason it didn't respond was because he hadn't figured out how to use it, simple as that. "How does it work then?"

"Periodic congruent entomological meta-euclidean adjacency."

Bert nodded all knowingly. "That's what I supposed. Better-included adjuicency."

"Meta-euclidean adjacency, Bert. You can pass through a non-congruent adjacency, but you can't connect its two aspects. It's only logical. Imagine the differential energy stored when a quarter of a gazillion miles of space-time is folded to less than a millimetre."

"Yeah, I can imagine. Have you ever tried folding a piece of paper nine times? Awesome, ain't it."

"Of course," said the Alien Father, "I'm no Doodad expert. You'll have to ask the Alien Mother for a detailed explanation."

"Look mate," said Bert, lips pinched together. "I don't need to ask the Alien Mother nothing. I understand all that babble perfectly. All I'm asking you is how to use the damn thing?"

"Do you have it?"

"Might have. Ain't saying. Just curious about how to turn it on."

The Alien Father stifled a scream. "The Doodad is so simple to operate a four-year-old could manage it."

"Yeah, but you'd have to show it how first."

"True, and since you don't have it, there's no point in me telling you."

Bert couldn't let on he'd found the Doodad. Not yet. If the Ewepiterians feared the Guardians would seize it and follow him back to Earth, they'd never let him use it. He let his shoulders slump. The Ewepitarians were a kind-hearted race of aliens who wanted to keep Earth safe, and he could only admire them. It just meant he'd have to find some way of pacifying them before he revealed the Doodad.

Problem solving wasn't one of Bert's strong points, but he realised he'd have to do something about those accursed Guardians. He needed more information about them. "I'd like a close up look at the Guardian's citadel. Will you take me?"

The Alien Father squeezed his eyes shut and his chin trembled. "No."

"Why not. You said you tried to organise a scouting expedition once. Why so frightened now?"

"Because... Because when I suggested it I knew nobody would go."

Bert slapped his knees and laughed. He liked the little man's honesty. "There ain't no danger. Show me the way, and when we get there you can hide behind a rock and watch."

The Alien Father clamped his hands over his ears and shook his head. "No. I daren't. They'll kill us."

"I ain't going to do nothing but spy on them. I'll hide with you, quiet as a mouse." Bert laced his fingers behind his head and whistled tunelessly. He wasn't as honest as the Alien Father, but telling believable lies was one of his strong points. "Eh, what do you say? After I've seen them, we'll scamper."

"Can't you ask somebody else to take you?"

"You're the bravest man here. When we get back, you'll be a hero."

The Alien Father pinched the bridge of his broad, flat nose. "You promise it's only for a quick peek?"

"I give you my word."

"Okay. Let's go before I change my mind. We start early in the morning, right after breakfast."

"Don't tell me," said Bert, so hungry he'd eat anything. "Bamboo shoot porridge."

***

By early afternoon next day, they'd scrambled along an overgrown path through the dense forest and advanced to higher ground. The air grew chilly, and the trees thinned enough to glimpse the Guardian's citadel, prominent on the hilltop. From a distance, it resembled a rotten black tooth, jagged at the top. A weird display of red lights danced in the sky above it, too distant to see details.

Bert and the Alien Father clambered the remaining way and kept hidden in the trees. They found a large boulder, big as a house, where they could stay out of sight and set up camp if necessary.

Beyond the rock they heard grinding music issue from the citadel's depths, crashing with fanfares of distorted hornpipes.

"Can we go now?" said the Alien Father.

"Not until I get a proper sight of them. Come on." Bert strolled boldly around the rock and through the last few trees until he drew close enough to see the citadel clearly. The Alien Father hid behind one of his legs, whimpering.

The Guardians had cleared an area the width of a soccer pitch around their citadel, the grass lush and well trimmed. Bert counted ten robot mowers trundling around the hill, manicuring the lawn. The stronghold was a simple structure of straight lines—a squat tower of four equally broad and high walls with no carvings or ornaments. It had no windows, heavy double doors on one wall, and was crowned with a sturdy battlement. The entire setup throbbed with latent power, giving Bert the impression it might come alive at any moment and gobble them.

A hellish red glow burst from the parapets and up into the air. Bert backed away, his heart pounding in his chest, and almost tripped over the Alien Father.

Neither of them spoke because just then a figure formed in the crimson bloom—the figure of a Guardian. Watching it made Bert dizzy, and when it turned to face him, he drew a stuttered gasp. Red glowing pinpricks appeared in the demonic face, swelled, and developed into eyes. The pupils were black chasms, pierced by volcanic pools of molten lava. Bert wanted to run, but those eyes held him. They radiated fury, loathing, and the hatred of a mad devil's soul.

Bert's blood thickened like syrup, and his scrotum tightened. The Guardian hung suspended in the air, nailing Bert with its burning gaze, and he knew his next breath would be his last.

Then the image faded, disappeared, and left the citadel in plain view. Bert swallowed, fought the urge to scamper, and waited to see what might happen next.

A moment later, small vehicles buzzed above the tower's top, like honeybees flitting in and out of their hive. They resembled flying mopeds without wheels, and they each towed a boxcar. The ones leavening were empty. Those that arrived contained ten children each, crying hysterically.

"They take children from the entire planet," said the Alien Father through gritted teeth.

Bert had forgotten about the Alien Father and was surprised he hadn't fainted or run off. "Why so few?"

"So few what?"

"Children."

"We calculate they take three-hundred thousand children each year. Is that so few?"

Bert gulped, ashamed of himself and his cruel, insensitive question. Boiling with fury at the Guardians, he clenched his jaw so tight it hurt. The Alien Father was angry too. Or was it fear? Bert couldn't tell.

A robot mower chomped its way past their hideout and the Alien Father shot out from behind his tree and kicked it. It rolled onto its back, wheels pointing to heaven. Trying to believe what he'd seen, Bert shook his head. There was no doubt the Alien Father boiled with anger, too. Bert rushed out, lifted the little man, and carried him back to safety. Not a moment too soon, because a door in the tower creaked open.

A creature stepped out. Behind it, Bert saw a Doodad placed in the centre of the citadel. Against the back wall, the air shimmered and the throat of a tunnel gaped open, the other end open on the Guardian's distant planet.

The creature had the body of a gorilla but stood erect and proud, like a commando soldier, half a head taller than Bert. And what an ugly head; it reminded Bert of a wild boar with tusks in its bottom jaw. Certain of its dominance over the meek Ewepitarians, it carried no weapon that Bert could see. The hideous brute strutted toward the upturned lawnmower and rectified it. Then it scanned all around with black, sallow eyes, piercing and cruel. Its snout sniffed like a dog on the scent of a bitch.

It occurred to Bert this was a genuine Guardian. The image in the air a projection designed to terrify the Ewepitarians and keep them away. He thought that was hardly necessary when the creature was so frightful anyway.

"Stay still and don't move," whispered Bert.

"Run," screeched the Alien Father, and bolted off down the hill.

"Crazy little twit," grumbled Bert, and chased after him. A glance over his shoulder revealed the Guardian catching up. "If you're going to run," puffed Bert. "You better go a lot faster or you'll be the main course at their next barbeque party."

The Alien Father's stumpy legs zipped along in a blur until he tripped and fell. Bert's body weight carried him on, and when he eventually stopped and turned, he saw the Guardian standing over the Alien Father with his boot raised, ready to stamp it down on his little friend's head.

"Hey!" shouted Bert. He grabbed a fist-sized boulder and hurled it at the Guardian. It struck it in the chest with enough force to make it lose balance and step back. The Alien Father squirmed to his feet and darted off down the hill, leaving Bert to face the Guardian.

Fury blazed in the Guardian's black eyes. It charged at Bert, outstretched arms clawing for Bert's face. Although Bert was shorter than the Guardian, he reckoned he was heavier and stronger. Every day, sometimes twice a day, he wrestled and boxed with his best mate, Alf. Alf was England's undisputed bare-fist street fighter champion. Rough stuff was an everyday part of Bert's life, and he knew many tricks.

Bert bent his knees slightly and balanced his body. He waited unmoving until the Guardian's claws were an inch from his nose. Then, in one smooth movement, he stepped aside, tripped it, and helped it on its flight by tugging an arm and kicking its backside.

The Guardian's head struck a tree trunk with a sickening crunch. Bert wasn't sure if the creature was dead or unconscious, and he didn't hang around to find out. Without a backward glance, he took off after the Alien Father.

***

"You're alive!" said the Alien Father as Bert burst into his house. He sat on a stool, head in hands, and genuine surprise in his voice. "What happened?"

"You should have stuck around instead of running off. Then you wouldn't need to ask."

The Alien Father let his head fall back into his palms. "It's my natural instincts. If I were big and strong like you I might have stayed, but measly and timid as I am, I fled."

Bert crawled across the floor on hands and knees, pivoted to sit beside the Alien Father, and reached his arm behind the midget's narrow back. "Can't blame you. I nearly did a runner myself."

The Alien Father sighed and glanced at Bert with a twitch of a smile. "You saved my life."

"Yes, well, the Guardian didn't put up much of a fight. I came on down right after you and I ain't sure whether it's dead or alive."

The Alien Father shrunk in terror. "We should never have gone. They'll come looking for us and kill us all."

"Yeah, that's what I dejuiced." Bert frowned. The Guardian he'd fought was a caretaker. If the creature lived and returned to the citadel, how soon would it raise the alarm and mobilize a squad of Guardians? If dead, when would its comrades miss it? The Guardians who came for Bert would be warriors: bigger, stronger, fiercer, and armed with ray guns. He doubted there was time to prepare a defence, and apart from his knife, he had no weapon. He didn't stand a chance.

His mind whirled. What should he do? Stay or return to Earth? He had little choice. He couldn't return to Earth because he couldn't work the Doodad. A doctor of physics might work it out, but Bert left school when he was fifteen. Or was he thrown out? He couldn't remember. So anyway, he'd have to stick around and fight to the death, making sure he took a few Guardians with him.

His thoughts went to his beloved Olive, who he'd never see again, and his best friend Alf, and his two Chums, the Alsatians, and his horse, Bigfoot. *Bye-bye, buddies.*

But then again, staying to fight was a stupid idea. He couldn't win a war by himself, he needed help, and that he'd find back on Earth. "You, Alien Father," said Bert, licking his lips with cautious hope. "We can't sit here and wait for the Guardians to slaughter us. Let's get the Doodad working and I'll pop back to my planet for help."

"I don't believe you'll come back."

"Come with me then. I'll round up me mates and a crate of dynamite and we'll be back in a jiffy. If we're quick enough, we'll blow the Guardian's citadel to smithereens."

"But suppose we're not quick enough and they destroy my village and then follow us to your planet?"

"All the more reason to hurry. Maybe the Guardian's caretaker was alone, the rest coming and going on their flying mopeds. It might give us time. Stop dilly-dallying and let's go."

The Alien Father inhaled deeply through the nose and then breathed out through the mouth. "If I were brave and strong like you, I'd help you against the Guardians." He clenched his little fists, bounced to his feet, and spread his legs. "I'd pound them into mush."

"Yeah, I reckon you would," said Bert. He sniffed. "The way I see it, you're so puny because of that rubbish you eat."

The Alien Father's display of bravery vanished as quickly as it came, and he slumped. "Bamboo shoots. It's our staple diet. It's all we have."

Bert wiggled his eyebrows and gave the Alien Father a friendly nudge, almost knocking him over. "Where I come from, there's a man named Popeye who grows super strong when he eats spinach."

"What breed of meat is spinach?"

"It's a vegetable, dark-green and leafy. It tastes almost as disgusting as your bamboo shoots. You'll love it. If you come back to my place, I'll fix a feast guaranteed to make you tough and strong."

"Without meat?"

"I promise."

"What's in it then?"

"Energy protein powder, which is made from soybeans, peas, potatoes and vegetables like that. I'll add some spinach and mix it all into a porridge with a liquid called vodka. It'll put hairs on your chest."

"Are you sure?"

"Positive. Hurry, we ain't got much time."

The Alien Father narrowed his eyes and squinted at Bert. "So you do have the Doodad. Where have you concealed it?"

"You're sitting on it."

Keeping one eye on Bert, the Alien Father peeked with his other eye under his cane chair and found the Doodad tied beneath with pieces of bamboo ribbon. "I knew you had it all the time." He eased it out, kissed it, and gave Bert a slow smile. "It's too cramped to use it in here. Let's take it outside."

In the open, Bert gazed about. The village seemed deserted. "Where is everyone?"

"When I told them what we'd done, they got scared again and rushed off back to the temple."

"Why didn't you go with them?"

The Alien Father sniffed and wiped at his nose. "They hate me for what we did. They don't think I'm a hero at all, like you said they would. 'Dumb agitator' is what they called me, and the Elder said I must sacrifice my life and hope the Guardians will settle for that."

"Ignore them," said Bert, desperate to leave for Earth. "They're a load of wimps. We'll show them heroes. Get the Doodad working."

"Let's hope you didn't break it. Are you ready?"

"Yeah." Bert watched intently, keen to learn how to turn it on.

"Place it on the ground," said the Alien Father. "This side up is off." He then turned it onto its other side. "And this side up is on."

Immediately, a shimmering haze formed above the gadget, hissing like a snake. In a few seconds, the tunnel's gaping mouth opened, all set to swallow them.

"Was it really that simple?" said Bert, scratching his bald head.

"Yes."

Bert didn't want to think about how unlucky he'd been, placing the Doodad in the off position every time he set it down. Still, he now knew how to operate it, and the knowledge made him smile. "Let's go."

The Alien Father dodged behind Bert. "You first. Dash into the tunnel full speed. That way, the dissolving experience is less formidable and you'll be through in seconds."

Bert took his advice, lowered his head, and charged into the tunnel's deep throat. A feather pillow slapped his face, another struck his back, and then he stumbled into number three, Flintstone Cottage, The Stables, London, England, Earth.

The Alien Father bumped into his legs, looked all around, eyes blinking rapidly, and rotated the Doodad into the off position. He shivered. "It's cold here."

After the sweaty tropical warmth of Ewepiter, Bert was glad. "Much better, don't you think?"

"No."

"It's because you haven't got any fat on you, but we'll soon put that straight." A quick glance told Bert everything was how he'd left it. Strange nobody came to see what had happened to him. "Let's go to my place. I'll light the fire and you'll soon warm up. Just don't poop in the sink."

"Is it far?"

"Two houses away."

"I'll bring the Doodad," said the Alien Father. "As long as it's turned off, the Guardians can't come through."

This was good, and Bert gave the 'thumbs-up'. Now he'd have the whole morning to fix the energy drink and round up weapons. He strode out into the backyard, headed along the alleyway past Olive's mid-terrace house, and stopped at his own residence at the terrace's other end. "Home-sweet-home," he mumbled.

By the sun's height, it was early morning, the same time of day he'd departed. How many days had he been away? He'd lost count. At least two.

His horse, Bigfoot, still saddled and tethered to the handle of his outside toilet, whinnied and pawed with his hoof. He could also hear his two Alsatians inside the house grow excited at his return. This was even stranger, hadn't anyone taken care of his pets while he'd been away?

Bigfoot nuzzled Bert's neck. "Ain't you let anyone close enough to take you back to the stable?" said Bert. He reached into his pocket for his phone and then recalled how the Alien Mother had smashed it for parts to repair the Doodad.

Now he'd have to borrow Olive's phone to find out why his best mate Alf hadn't looked after his pets. That's if she could find it, or the battery wasn't flat like normal, or she hadn't dropped it in the bath again. He wondered what Olive had been up to while he'd been away. Most likely taken the opportunity to go off flirting. But then he noticed her back door slightly open, a sure sign she was up and about.

Bert hugged Bigfoot's neck and whispered in his ear. "Sorry I've been gone for so long. It won't happen again. I love you, mate."

To his astonishment, his horse said, "I love you too, mate." Bert shook his head. The journey between planets must have jangled his brain.

The Alien Father reached out and stroked Bigfoot's knee.

"Don't he scare you?" said Bert, eyebrows raised. Hardly anyone was brave enough to touch his horse, and his horse seldom allowed anybody to approach him.

"He's like me, a grazer, a hunted animal, but so proud, so strong."

"Yeah, he's a good friend," said Bert. "So are you, and I don't eat my friends. We'll soon have you just as strong as Bigfoot." He waggled a finger in his ear. "I don't suppose you've ever seen a horse. We've got loads of animals here on Earth. Come inside and meet me Chums."

"Chums?"

"Yeah, me Alsatians. Two little fluff balls. They're dogs. Can't understand why, but everybody seems scared stiff of them."

Bert's Alsatians sniffed him suspiciously. "Where've you been, Boss? Where've you been?" he heard them say. "You smell funny. Take us with you next time, we'll protect you. Who's that with you? Shall we kill him?"

Bert shook his head again and wondered how long it would take before his brain settled. "This is my friend." He reached behind his back and yanked the Alien Father into view. "Say hello to him—nicely!" His Chums moved closer to the Alien Father, sniffed at the strange little creature, and growled deep in their throats.

"They're meat-eaters," said the Alien Father. He scrunched his eyes shut and was so rigid he trembled.

"Tasty!" said Bert's Chums.

"Out of bounds," said Bert. "Go to your corner and don't even look at him."

They slinked off, ears plastered flat against their heads.

Bert pulled the Alien Father with him into the lounge. Two bulky-stuffed armchairs squatted on each side of the open fire, and a well-cushioned settee stretched along the furthest wall. A light beige carpet covered the floor. Sitting on the mantelpiece, a clock ticked lazily, and above that on the chimney breast hung a large picture of an angel with tears in her eyes. Dogs' hairs coated everything.

An even bigger surprise greeted Bert. Someone had lit his fire and the logs blazed cheerfully, just like when he'd hurried away to visit the newcomer dwarf at number three all those days ago.

"Sit in that armchair next to the fire and warm yourself," said Bert. "Olive's been here, bless her. Put the Doodad by your feet where it's safe. We don't want Olive tinkering with it." He gave a little wink. "Women!"

Bert nudged his chair closer to the warmth and threw in two logs. The Alien Father tugged and pushed his armchair, but he was too weak to budge it. So Bert reached across, dragged it for him, and scooted him into the cushions head first. "And now," said Bert, rubbing his hands, "I'm going to make you my 'Piss De Resistant.' "

While the Alien Father toasted his hands, Bert set about making his special porridge. He found a large basin and dumped in one giant mug of oat-based instant-breakfast cereal and three mugs of energy protein powder. It needed one full bottle of vodka to mix it into a thin gruel. Then he added an eggcup of salt, a teacup of sugar, and a tin of Popeye spinach. Three minutes in the microwave made it pleasantly warm and thick.

He carried the porridge, two cereal bowls, two spoons, and a jar of honey back into the lounge and set them on the floor between the armchairs. After making himself comfortable, he spooned porridge into one bowl, smothered it in honey, raisins and sliced banana, and handed it to the Alien Father. Then he filled his own dish.

The Alien Father dipped the tip of his spoon into the porridge and tasted it carefully. Bert watched with keen attention; his own spoonful halted in front of his mouth. The Alien Father's eyebrows shot up and a smile exploded across his face. "This is good," he said and spooned porridge as if he hadn't eaten for a week.

Happy that his experiment worked out so well, Bert gobbled his own bowlful. To his surprise, the Alien Father ate his just as fast. Bert refilled both bowls. Compared to the bamboo tips porridge he'd choked on lately, and even though he'd rather have a slab of bloody beef, his own vegan creation was heaven.

When he reached to fill the bowls for a third time, he saw the Alien Father had fallen asleep, his dish and spoon nestled on his swollen belly. Reckoning his alien friend wouldn't want more, Bert finished the rest, eating straight from the basin.

Two minutes later, stomach full, head spinning, comfy and warm in front of the fire, the threat of the Guardians forgotten, Bert fell asleep too.

***

In the house adjoining Bert's, Olive finished her fifth cup of tea and yawned. Today, she'd set her alarm to ring at nine in the morning: the middle of the night for her! She wasn't an early riser like her fiancé, Bert, and she wasn't a nosy person either, but she fidgeted to learn what Bert had found out about the strange dwarfs at number three.

After she'd showered and applied her make-up, she'd opened the back door of her house. Bert would then realise she was up, and come in to tell her his news. She'd noticed his horse parked outside his house, so she knew he was there.

Olive wasn't keen on animals, and she'd never had a pet. Bert's Alsatians and his horse frightened the life out of her, especially the stallion: big docile man and his bigger wild horse. Sometimes, she thought Bert loved his animals more than he loved her. God knows he spent more time with his pets than with her.

By now, it was noon, her normal waking time. In another hour she'd have to leave for work, sorting The Stable's financial books. She pounded her fist against the kitchen table, making her teacup and saucer jump. Why hadn't Bert come with his gossip?

Frustration kicked in, and she dumped her cup and saucer in the stone sink so carelessly the cup's handle snapped off. A wave of fury crashed through her. Since Bert was so selfish and uncaring that he didn't see fit to pop in, then she'd go to his house. And she'd make sure the big lout regretted the day he was born.

Not daring to go near the horse, and knowing Bert kept his ferocious dogs in the living room, Olive burst into Bert's house by the front door. She stormed straight into the lounge. The air stunk of alcohol and Bert's deep snoring made her wish she'd brought some cotton wool; either to put in her ears or stuff down his throat. He slouched in his favourite armchair, arms dangling over the rests, feet almost in the fire that still glowed warmly.

In the opposite chair slept a dwarf. He was tiny, but had muscles like a bodybuilder, straining against his clothes so tightly she marvelled at how he'd ever put them on.

Between them on the floor was a gadget that pulsed with a dull glow.

Olive's lips thinned. Momentarily fascinated, she plucked the gadget up for a closer look. It was about the size of a lunch box, made of two metal plates sandwiching an inch thick layer of jelly. Inside the jelly floated odd-shaped bits and pieces, some of them glowing faintly in various colours, swimming around like miniature fish.

She thought it would look perfect in her bathroom, alongside the candles and glass of wine, glimmering in all those gorgeous colours while she meditated in the bath. So she tossed it on the sideboard close to the door. On her way out, she'd take it with her.

"Wake up, you fat pig," she screamed at Bert. He smiled and grunted, but didn't wake. The dwarf, however, did. My God, he seemed drunk, because his two eyes rotated in all directions and he spoke some gibberish that sounded like backwards Arabian.

Ignoring him, she bent over Bert and prised his eyelids open with her green-manicured fingernails. "Bert. Wake up. What's going on here? Why haven't you come to my house? Who's this?"

Bert groaned and held his eyes open without Olive's help. "Oh, my head," he grunted, and then smiled as he recognised her. "Hi, Olive. Lovely to see you again. What day is it?" It sounded as though his tongue flopped around inside his mouth like a wet sponge.

"Who's that?" Olive pointed at the Herculean dwarf.

"Ah, him. He's called Alien Father, and he's from a town called Lambden on a planet called Ewepiter."

Olive's nostrils flared. Not only had Bert ignored her when he returned from number three, but now he mocked her. "And what's this gadget?" she snatched up the glowing sandwich and shoved it under Bert's nose.

Bert squinted at it and scratched his battered ear. "Better be careful with that. It's a Doodad that opens a tunnel across the universe and works on the principle of Better-European Idiocy."

"Meta-Euclidean Adjacency," corrected the Alien Father, flexing his biceps and gazing at them with eyes as wide as saucers.

"What did he say?" asked Olive.

"He said what I said." Bert gave a shaky laugh. "Oh, yeah, I forgot, you ain't got a universal translator like what I've got." He patted the gleaming badge on his sweat-stained T-shirt. "You can't hear him like what I can. I can even speak to me Chums and me horse now. Want me to translate?"

Olive didn't understand why Bert was talking to her like this, and she didn't like it. She didn't know whether she should box his ears or phone for an ambulance to take him away to the funny farm. She spun and headed for the door. "When you're sober, you can come and apologise. And you better make it good."

She didn't realise she still clasped the gadget until she was safely in her own house again. It had lost its charm for her; whatever it was, she hated it. She opened her back door and flung it into her garden. It bounced twice, rolled along on its thin sides, and stopped in the middle of her lawn, teetering on edge. A puff of wind nudged it. It fell, on side up, and the tunnel opened, breaching the way for the dreaded Guardians.

***

With Olive out of his face and out of his house, Bert ogled the Alien Father with amazement. The little man's muscles bulged. "You feeling alright?" he asked.

"No, my skin is too tight." He stretched this way and that, groaning with pleasure as he flexed his swollen muscles. "Your mixture. It works. We must return to Ewepiter without delay so I can crush the Guardians."

"Now you just hold on a minute there," said Bert. "You might be a mite stronger, but you're still a little squirt. You ain't no match for the Guardians. And I don't suppose you're any braver either."

The Alien Father slumped back into his chair. "You are right. The idea of meeting a Guardian makes me sick in the stomach."

"Give me your hand and squeeze mine with all you've got."

The Alien Father reached across and grasped three of Bert's fingers. The muscles in the alien's arms twisted into knots as he gritted his teeth. Bert had felt stronger hands on the older children at the stables, trying to prise a coin from his clenched fist.

Bert shook the Alien's hand off and offered him a walnut. "Let's see if you can crush this before you start on the Guardians." Again, the alien's muscles bunched, but the nut didn't crack. Bert gave him another. "Here, try this one. Use both hands." This time, the nut popped and crumbled. "Good, now eat what you find inside. It's full of protein." He took the harder nut from the Alien Father, crushed it open between finger and thumb, and tossed the kernel into his mouth.

The Alien Father stopped chewing his nut. His jaws tensed. One of his eyes swivelled around the room; the other glared at the floor between them. "The Doodad," he gasped. "It's gone..."

"You stashed it under your chair," said Bert, hardly paying attention. He had another matter on his mind. "There's one goings-on I don't understand. I've been on your planet for two days, but time hasn't changed here. It's like I slipped away half an hour ago and just got back."

"The Doodad also bends time," said the Alien Father, crawling around the floor on hands and knees.

Cogwheels turned in Bert's brain. Bent time: what was that supposed to mean? "So, while we're here, do you mean time isn't running on your planet?"

"Yes, of course, but the Doodad returns us almost to the moment we left. If we were away for ten years, the others would see we'd grown old in minutes."

"Got you." Bert's head ached from the alcohol and his stomach rumbled with hunger again. "Why?"

"Why what?"

"Why would we look ten years older?"

The Alien Father stopped his crawling and gazed up at Bert. "Because time continues simultaneously in both worlds whether the tunnel is open or not."

"Oh." Bert's concentration shattered and his posture collapsed. To make sense, he needed to draw a diagram. Just as he half rose to fetch a pencil and pad, the Alsatians growled; a deep menacing sound in their throats. "What is it, Chums?"

"Intruder. Coming. Evil. Kill it. Intruder. Kill it..."

Bert laughed out loud. "I love the way you guys talk to me."

"Danger. Boss. Intruder. Outside. Kill it."

The Alien Father had lost interest in Bert. He tugged at the armchairs and peered beneath them, his new muscles flexing and heaving. "The Doodad," he called, panic in his voice. "Where is it?"

Bert thought about it. The answer was simple. "Olive took it with her."

They gaped at each other, horror in their eyes, and the Alsatians howled so fiercely that Bert couldn't figure out a bark they said. All he knew is that something dreadful outside was happening.

A piercing scream reached them from somewhere out back. Bert could recognise Olive's exquisite voice anywhere. For one reason or another she often screamed, especially at him. Ah, she was a fiery little lady at times, and Bert loved her for it. This time, Bert could tell she was genuinely terrified, and his heart missed a beat.

Then, to make matters worse, his horse brayed and stamped. Fearing the worse, Bert lurched to his feet. To his surprise, the Alien Father beat him to it and darted past him out through the back door.

"Come on, Chums," said Bert as he followed the little man.

"Kill, kill, kill!" snarled the Alsatians, vaulting through the back door before Bert.

The Alien Father hadn't gone far. He hid behind a coal bunker, no sign of his bravery now. Bert glanced past him, and what he saw made his heart leap into his mouth, making it impossible to speak. In the middle of Olive's lawn, the tunnel between planets gaped open, hissing and throbbing like a maelstrom from hell.

A massive Guardian stood there, two heads taller than Bert's six-foot-five, shoulders half-a-metre broader than the biggest gorilla he'd seen at London Zoo. Olive's unconscious body flopped over one of its arms like a rag doll. It clasped a ray gun in its other hand, its glossy shape looking just like a kid's fancy water pistol.

Bert didn't know what plans the Guardian had for Olive, but seeing her in such danger drove him insane. Fury vibrated through his being. Almost choking with rage, he bent his head, clenched his hands into fists of granite, and charged.

When the Guardian saw him coming, a smirk creased its large jaw muscles, exposing broad, strong teeth. The mocking laughter dumped hot coals into the pit of Bert's belly, super-charging his headlong rush.

The Guardian raised its ray gun coolly and pointed it at Bert.

In the event of guns pointing in their direction, Bert had trained his Alsatians to rush in from the side and attack the assailant's arm. They didn't let him down. Only feet away from the beast, both dogs clamped their teeth onto the Guardian's forearm and wrist. It roared, threw Olive aside, and used its free arm to swipe at the dogs. Despite the animal's enormous size, compared to the Guardian, they looked no larger than miniature poodles. But they'd locked their jaws, and although the Guardian lifted both from the ground and wrenched at their necks, they held tight.

Head first, Bert crashed full speed into the Guardian's stomach. Its belly felt as solid as a punch bag and Bert heard his neck creak. But the beast gave a blast of air and toppled over, ray gun skidding across the lawn. "Throat," said Bert, and his dogs dropped the arm and went for its neck. In the same instant, Bert darted to his horse and tried to vault onto its back like he'd seen in the movies. His gut bounced into Bigfoot's rump, but he grabbed the saddle, pulled himself up, and slid his feet into the stirrups.

The Guardian was on its feet again. Blood poured from its torn arm, but it still had enough strength to wrench at the dogs and protect its hairy throat. Fearing for the safety of his pets, Bert roared a command at them. "Stand away, Chums."

High in the horse's saddle, Bert towered above the guardian. Beneath him, Bigfoot vibrated with energy and anger. Bert swung the stallion and gave a signal to kick with its hind legs. With enough force to punch a hole through a barn wall, Bigfoot's hooves crashed into the Guardian's chest at the speed of two-hundred miles per hour.

Bert heard bones crack, then saw the guardian fly backwards and disappear into the tunnel he'd come from.

Olive lay sprawled on the lawn, unconscious, but still breathing. Hot tears flooded Bert's eyes. All of this was his fault, a result of his dumb, meddling stupidity. To see his beloved fiancé in such a sad state was more than his heart could bear, and it fluttered in his chest like an Ostrich with a knot in its neck.

The Alien Father rushed from hiding and plunged head first into the throbbing tunnel, back to his own world. There was no time for Bert to reflect on whether he should stay and tend to Olive, or have it out with the Guardians. With a soft nudge from his heels, Bigfoot reared on its hind legs and then charged into the tunnel's mouth, his Chums running beside him.

The shift between planets happened so fast it seemed no worse than jumping through a loop, a trick he'd often practised with Bigfoot. The abrupt switch of scenery, however, spooked the horse, and it took all Bert's coaxing to halt his gallop. "It's alright," soothed Bert, stroking the animal's neck. "It's a new trick. Sorry, I should've warned you."

"New trick," snorted Bigfoot. "Okay, let's do it again."

"Later," said Bert. "Work first."

Back outside the Alien Father's house, the defeated Guardian slumped against a wall, its chest caved in, dead. Bert dropped from his horse and called his Chums to his side. A quick search revealed their bodies covered in bumps and bruises, but no bones broken or severe cuts.

The Alien Father had already turned the Doodad into the 'off' position, closing the tunnel and stopping Earth time. A wave of relief passed through Bert. Back home,

Olive lay prone on the lawn, and when he returned, if ever he did, he wanted her still lying there, where he could care for her.

"The Guardian was alone," said the Alien Father. "But others will come. What shall we do?"

Bert wasn't good at taking charge and giving orders. He usually let his best mate, Alf, do that. He tilted his head from side to side, weighing choices. "I think you should hide the Doodad and join the villagers at the Temple where it's safe."

"What about you?"

Before answering, Bert tugged on his bottom lip. "Well, I'm going to the Guardian's citadel." He wasn't sure what he'd do when he arrived, but it seemed the obvious move.

"Take me with you. Mount your magnificent beast, make room for me, and pull me up."

Bert's mouth fell open. "You want to come too?"

"Yes. Just give me a second to hide the Doodad."

Bert blew into the nostrils of his horse and stroked its long neck. "Be brave, my friend," he breathed. "Remember the tricks we've practised, we'll need them now."

The horse nodded. "I remember. You want me to fight. I understand. You and me. Fight."

"Good," said Bert. "You, me, our Chums, and the Alien Father. The magnificent five versus the curse of the universe: the Guardians."

The horse trotted, reserving its energy, but they covered distance fast. As they neared the forest edge that hemmed the Guardian's citadel, Bert stopped, lowered the Alien Father to the ground, and dropped to his side.

"Back on my planet," said Bert, "we have animals called sheep. They're a lot like you, docile, but not half as brainy. We call the male sheep rams and they can be aggressive. Some have caused serious injuries, even death, to people." He placed his hand on the Alien Father's shoulder and fixed him with a stare. "I'm asking you to be a ram. Can you do it?"

"I won't run away this time," said the Alien Father, tightening his impressive muscles.

"Good."

"We have to take the Guardians by surprise."

"Yeah, that's what I reckon, too. Got any ideas?"

The Alien Father gave a curt nod and answered with a steady low-pitched voice. "I'll stay here and count to a hundred while you sneak closer. Then I'll kick one of their lawnmowers again and draw their attention. When they come out of the citadel to chase me, you go in. How about that?"

"Got it. Count to one hundred." It wasn't much of a plan, thought Bert, and he didn't want the Alien Father hurt. But if the little fellow was brave enough to do his part, and then run off, good. He'd take care of the rest. "Here, take my knife. It'll give you courage."

The Bowie Knife looked like a sabre in the Alien Father's grip. The tip rested on the ground. "Don't you need it?"

"I've got another one," said Bert. It was a lie, and he almost changed his mind. "Why didn't you take the ray gun back on my planet? It was on the lawn. You almost tripped over it."

"Why didn't you?"

Not wanting to start an argument, Bert spurred Bigfoot and rode off. He stopped when he faced the citadel's doors, keeping out of sight in the trees. Right on cue, the Alien Father darted out and booted a lawnmower onto its back.

Instead of retreating into the trees, as Bert expected, the Alien Father sprinted across the neatly cut grass and kicked another lawnmower onto its side.

The citadel's double doors cracked open, and a huge Guardian emerged, wielding a ray gun. The Alien Father whirled about, bent over to touch his toes, and let his guts unleash a riot of gas. Produced from his unusual meal and extreme nervousness, it sounded like a long sharp military blast from a bugle.

"You measly little turd," roared the Guardian as it charged, "You'll pay for that with a boot up your arse."

"Now," said Bert, and sent Bigfoot bolting across the lawn. The Guardian skidded and stopped, undecided which way to run. Seeing Bert on horseback and two savage dogs rushing for the citadel door, it wheeled around and raced back.

Galloping at full speed, Bert reached the citadel first and bolted inside. The space was as large as a tennis court, and the Guardian's Doodad rested on a low plinth in the centre of the uninhabited space. A tunnel swirled and wheezed, open to the Guardian's planet of evil.

"Stamp on it," shouted Bert into the horse's ear, and one second later a front hoof found its mark, smashing the gadget into a trillion pieces. In a flash, the tunnel collapsed, closed for ever.

Behind him, the Guardian scowled in the doorway, ray gun raised, temper foaming from the corners of its fat lips.

Bert cursed. He'd been careless. He should have set his dogs on the ugly creature. It had them trapped, too far away to reach before it pulled the trigger. A fearful gnarl creased the Guardian's brow as its finger squeezed.

In that same moment, a glint of steel flashed. The Alien Father inched up behind the Guardian, both hands clasping the razor-sharp Bowie knife above his head. His face was red and blotchy as if he'd been holding his breath, which then exploded from his mouth as he drove the knife into the back of the Guardian's thigh.

The Guardian gasped, eyes suddenly as wide as jam tarts cooling on a windowsill, and it swatted its leg as if a hornet had stung it.

That was all the time Bert needed. His horse and dogs reached the stunned Guardian and bowled it over. The

Alsatians tore at its throat, and a well-placed front hoof caved its skull in.

There was no joy for Bert in the victory. He was a 'has been' burglar, not a murderer. His arms fell limp by his sides, his chin trembled, and his voice dropped almost to a whisper. "It's over, Rambi, you can come out."

The Alien Father peeked around the door frame. Seeing the Guardian lying there, he tiptoed into view, sunk to his knees, and clasped his hands over his face. "You did it," he muttered through his fingers. "You closed the Guardian's tunnel. They can never come here again."

"Without you, Rambi, it would have cost my life. You're my hero." Bert dragged his knife from the fallen Guardian and handed it hilt first to the Alien Father. "Keep it. It's yours."

A bloom of red spread across the Alien Father's cheeks. Then an assured smile crossed his face, and he wagged his head up and down. "Rambi?"

"Yep. From now on I'll call you Rambi. It's a proper name, like Rambo and Bambi."

"You saved my life, now I've saved yours. Were Quits."

"We're buddies," said Bert, "and if we were on Earth, I'd take you to the pub for a beer." The Alien Father looked at him quizzically, his posture rigid. "It's a drink made from hops and barley. You'll love it,"

Above them, the terrifying projected image and trumpet sound continued. "I'll soon stop that," said Bert, scanning for the source.

"No, leave it!"

Bert didn't understand but was happy to let Alien Father take charge. "Why?"

"Guardians are still on my planet, rounding up our children. If you interrupt the projection, they'll realise something is wrong. Best to take them unawares."

As if to prove his point, a flying scooter appeared over the top of the citadel and slowly descended. The Alien Father snatched up the dropped ray gun, waited until the Guardian landed, and pulled the trigger. A dazzling zap pummelled the Guardian, and it burst into fizzing flames.

They released the children, dragged the remains of the scooter and its carriage into the forest, told the petrified kids to dash down to the village, and hid while they waited for the next Guardian to arrive.

"You'll be here a while, doing this," said Bert, impressed at the Alien Father's newfound confidence. "You don't need my help for a while. I'll be back shortly."

Five hours later, Bert returned to the rock camp, his horse and dogs panting. On the way, he'd passed several groups of children, tear-stained, yelping, plunging down the hill as swift as their stubby little legs would carry them. He found the Alien Father behind their rock camp, squatting on hands and knees, where he'd been sick.

"Hey, Rambi." Bert helped the dwarf to his feet and moved him farther behind the rock, where the trees provided shade and the air was cool. "Stomach puking up that strange food I gave you?"

The Alien Father shook his head. "No, not the food. It's this slaying."

"Yeah." Words stuck in Bert's throat and he wished he could relieve his friend's misery. He sat beside him and tugged him into a hug. "Want me to take over?"

"No. You've done enough. I have to prevail alone." The Alien Father sniffed, freed himself from Bert's massive arms, and thrust out his chest. He pointed to a stack of ray guns. "See. I've been collecting them. I'll not run out of firepower."

"You won't be alone for long." Bert told him he'd spoken to the Elder and disclosed all that had happened. In a wave of jubilation, the Elder had promised to send a small group of young men to help the Alien Father, with plenty of supplies for a lengthy campaign.

Words stuck in Bert's throat. His next piece of information stirred mixed emotions. "I've brought the Doodad with me. You're useless at hiding it. I'm going home. For ever."

A groan accompanied the roll of the Alien Father's eyes, making Bert want to hurry, to avoid the sadness of departure.

"When I get home, I'll smash the Doodad at my end, but don't turn your end off until the tunnel closes. I've got a present for you." With that, Bert, Bigfoot, and the Chums torpedoed themselves into the tunnel.

***

Olive still lay prostrate on the lawn, whimpering, her limbs giving a brief twitch every so often. Bert closed the tunnel, slipped the Doodad into a saddlebag on his horse, and knelt beside his beloved.

At the same moment, Florence, Chief Inspector Dobbs, and Vicar Bitter came ambling into view. When they saw Olive and Bert, they rushed.

"What has happened here?" demanded Chief Inspector Dobbs.

"Has this anything to do with the devil-worshipping dwarfs at number three?" said Vicar Bitter.

"You men are hopeless," said Florence, shaking her head. "Call for the doctor and help me get Olive inside."

Certain Olive was taken good care of, Bert sneaked off to his own house. He fed his dogs, tied Bigfoot to the outside toilet handle with a bale of straw at his feet, and hurried indoors. In the middle of his lounge, he opened the tunnel and tossed all his supplies of energy powder, spinach, and vodka into it. As a special treat, he sent a thirty pack of Fuller's ESB Ale.

Then he closed the tunnel, dropped the Doodad back into the horse's saddlebag, and joined the others at Olive's house next door. Olive rested on the sofa, a wet cloth on her brow and Florence sitting beside her, stroking her hand.

The men sat at the kitchen table, laden with cold meats and pickles, cheese and crusty bread. Bert knew Olive had made the snack for him; she was the sweetest woman on Earth. The sight of it made his mouth water, but he couldn't eat until Olive was better. Until then, he'd never eat again. "How is she?" he asked, wringing his hands.

"Nothing broken," said Florence, "but she's delirious. She keeps mumbling about alien monsters."

Bert gave a short, disgusted snort. "When I found her on the lawn, she talked about little men with wonky eyes and bulging muscles from another planet. Can't understand why people believe in aliens. They must be daft."

Vicar Bitter's mouth was full of food, so he said nothing, but nodded in agreement. Chief Inspector Dobbs paused with a sandwich in front of his mouth. "What did you find out about the midgets at number three?"

"Oh, yeah, them. Nothing. They were gone when I got there. Vanished."

Half the sandwich disappeared into Chief Inspector Dobbs' mouth. "So why," he uttered, spitting crumbs, "is Olive in the state she's in?"

"My guess is food poisoning," said Bert. "That meat you're eating smells off. You two'll soon be babbling about ghosts and spooks, just like her. I think we should all become vegetarians, that's what I think."

Vicar Bitter dashed from the room, hand clamped over his mouth, headed for the outside toilet. Chief Inspector Dobbs swallowed noisily and shoved his plate away. "I think I'll pop home. Florence, will you stay with Olive?"

"Of course. And when the doctor has finished here, I'll send him to check on you and Vicar Bitter."

In the days that followed, when life settled back into its everyday routine and Olive had fully recovered, Bert took the Doodad and translator badge to his bosses at The Cloud Mansion. The young masters often spoke of their adventures into outer space. They'd know what to do with his alien gadgets. Himself, he wanted nothing more to do with them. He'd experienced a space adventure of his own, but he kept it to himself. To this day, in memory of his friend Rambi, apart from a sausage now and then that hardly contains meat these days, he remains a vegetarian.

The end

Afterword

I hope you enjoyed this novella. If so, do me a favour by spreading the word on your Blog, Twitter or Facebook site. Why not let me and others know what you think by posting a review. It doesn't have to be much; even a few words are helpful. Thank you. James

ISBN-978-82-93174-79-0

Evil Portent

This novelette is a work of fiction.